DIGGER'S MATE

HELEN LUNN

illustrated by
CLIFTON PUGH

AIRD BOOKS

It was a mid summer's evening. The sun had
finished work for the day and the moon would
soon rise to take her place in the sky. A kingfisher
was flying home to its nest. Kookaburras laughed
and cicadas began their evening song, calling
the night-time animals to wake up one by one.

The wombat, already awake, was hungry. In her pouch, her baby wriggled. She was hungry too.

Mother wombat trundled up the track looking for food. She came to the road. She did not stop to look. She did not see the old bus speeding round the bend.

The kingfisher called 'Look out!' but it was too late.

Mother wombat rolled to the side of the road. She lay quite still.

A little gecko gave a sad cry and scurried into the bushes.

Joyce and her dog, Digger, were out for their morning walk. Joyce loved animals and she kept the bush around her house natural so that all the wild creatures would stay.

Digger saw the wombat first, and barked excitedly. But, as they drew nearer, both realised that the wombat was dead, and there was nothing they could do to help her.

Digger was quiet as Joyce knelt beside the poor, still creature and sadly stroked her fur.

Then something moved!

Looking very carefully inside the wombat's pouch, Joyce found the baby wombat, weak but still alive.

Digger became excited again and Joyce said softly, "Shhhh, Digger, you'll frighten her. Let's take her home."

Joyce named the baby wombat 'Myrtle'. She was very small and very pink, for she had not yet grown any fur. She shivered, fretting for the warm comfort of her mother.

Joyce talked to her friends at the animal sanctuary about caring for Myrtle. As they suggested, Joyce made Myrtle a pouch. Finding an old jumper, Joyce knotted the sleeves and sewed up the neck. On fine days she would hang the pouch on a line outside.

Digger wanted to help too. He sang a song for Myrtle. But it didn't sound like a song, it sounded like a dog barking, so Joyce told him to be quiet.

Digger was offended. He thought he had a very good singing voice.

Digger was watching through the lounge-room
window as Joyce fed Myrtle special milk through
an eye-dropper, then gently placed her, sleepy
and full, back in the jumper pouch.

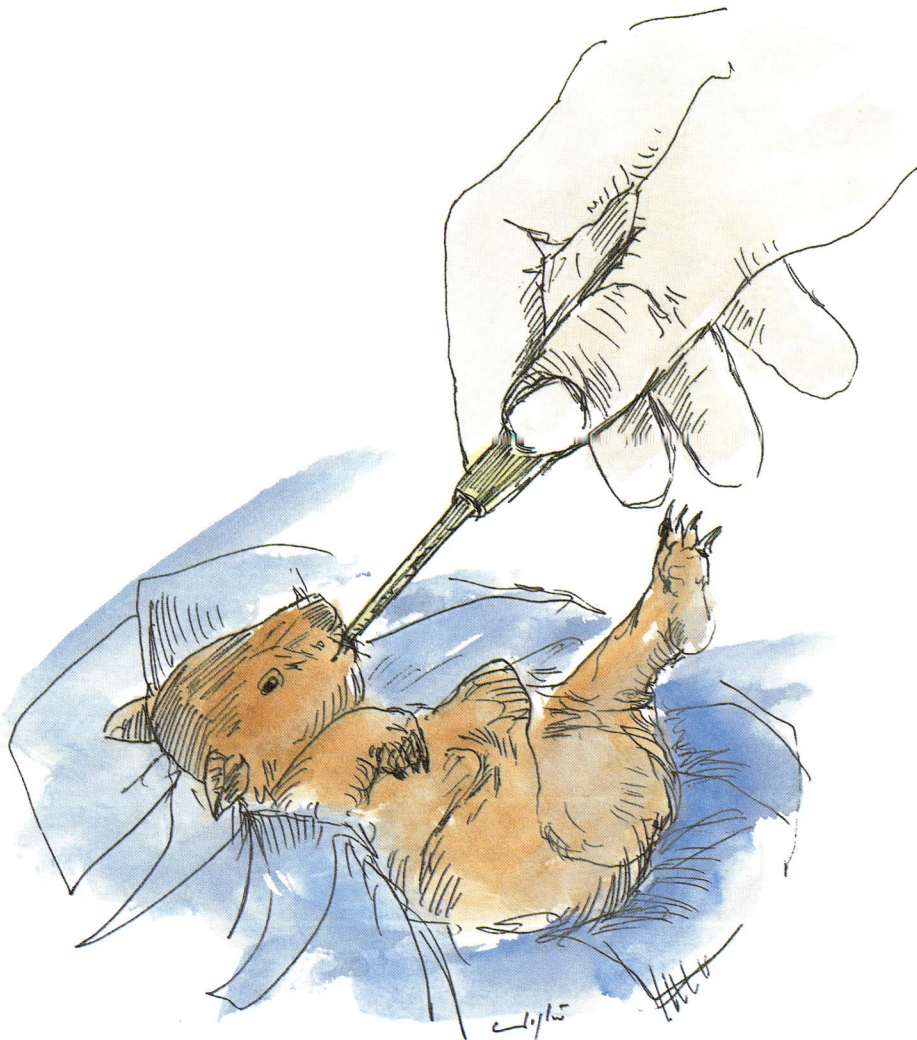

A handsome dragonfly hovered down to say hello. He tried to land on the ledge beside Digger, but missed, and ended up on top of him.

"Get off my head please," muttered Digger, not amused.

"Whoops!" Dragonfly hummed, straightening out his wings, "I'm great on take-offs but not so good on landings."

Dragonfly darted down and crash-landed on the ledge. "What's the matter with you, Digger?"

"Myrtle's the matter with me."

"Pardon?" asked Dragonfly.

"A baby wombat," sulked Digger.

"A baby wombat!" exclaimed Dragonfly. "I love baby wombats."

"I don't!" Digger's ears flattened against his head.

"Don't be such a sook," buzzed Dragonfly, whizzing away to tell his friends the news.

The animals who lived in the bush nearby watched as Myrtle grew stronger day by day. Before long she had fur – and teeth, and claws.

"She's going to be all right," hummed Dragonfly.

"She's sweet," chirped Gecko.

"She bites me when Joyce isn't looking," grumbled Digger.

"Myrtle only wants to play with you," said Gecko, searching for some shade.

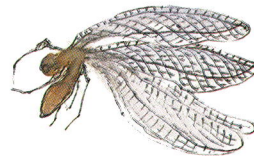

Digger sniffed. "You know, ever since that Myrtle arrived, Joyce hasn't had any time to play with me. She hasn't even had time to give me a bath."

"Yes, you do pong a bit," said Gecko. "When did you last have one?"

Digger had to think for a long time. "Was it Christmas?"

"Pooh!" exclaimed Dragonfly, "months ago." He took off into the sky, did a fantastic loop-the-loop and disappeared.

Digger looked round for Gecko, but she had gone too. "It's a dog's life," he whispered sadly to the world.

It was a rainy day towards the end of winter. Myrtle was trying out her new teeth and claws – on Joyce's furniture, floors and doors.

"If I did that," thought Digger, watching through the window, "I'd be in big trouble. It's not fair!" He rolled over onto his back, stuck his legs in the air and shut his eyes tight.

"Excuse me?" came a small voice. "May I enquire what you are doing?" A worm had taken advantage of the soggy day and was lounging about in the long grass.

"I'm playing dead," whispered Digger. "Joyce will take notice of me if she thinks I'm dead."

Worm gave a big yawn. "Don't be a silly duffer, you've got a wet nose."

"So?" asked Digger.

"Everyone knows a sick dog has a dry nose."

"How would you know?" Digger retorted.

Worm raised himself to his full height (which impressed a passing ant) and replied, "Because I am a bookworm!" With that, he wriggled off to the nearest puddle, did a beautiful belly-whacker and sank proudly to the bottom.

Digger marched over to the puddle. "And I am not a Silly Duffer," he called, head up and tail in the air. "I am a Kelpie Cross!"

Digger was in his kennel, concentrating on making his nose go dry. From the corner of his eye he noticed Myrtle asleep in her jumper pouch on the lawn.

He crept up to the jumper and started dragging the sleeping Myrtle towards the path. He was nearly there when Dragonfly nose-dived down, buzzing "What are you doing with Myrtle?"

"Taking her up to the neighbours' house," grumbled Digger. "They like wombats."

"But you and Myrtle could be friends," said Dragonfly. "Can't you share your home?"

"This is *my* home," replied Digger, "and we don't have room for strays." He continued to drag Myrtle across the yard – until he bumped into a pair of shoes.

Myrtle, who had quite enjoyed the ride, poked her head out of the jumper and gave Digger and Joyce a big wombat grin.

Joyce smiled down at them. "I'm glad to see you two having fun."

Digger was nearly sick!

Digger was in a particularly bad mood. Myrtle had dug up his favourite bone. He decided he would feel better if he chewed up Joyce's slippers.

Halfway through the second one she caught him. Angrily, she ordered him outside.

Digger wandered sadly among the daffodils. "Joyce doesn't love me any more. I'm going to run away."

"Where will you go?" asked the tallest daffodil, the spokesflower for the group.

"To Melbourne," replied Digger. "Somebody might want me in the big city."

"But what about Joyce?" chorused the daffodils. "She'll be lonely without you – and the city can be a big, cold place."

"She doesn't need me; she's got Myrtle."

"No, no, no!" exclaimed the daffodils, "Myrtle doesn't belong to Joyce. Joyce is just looking after Myrtle until she is big enough to look after herself. Then she will go back to the bush where she belongs. No one owns the wild things."

But Digger wasn't listening. He had gone off to his kennel to pack his swag. He wrapped his dish and his rubber bone in his dog blanket. He said goodbye to his mate, the stink beetle, who had been his friend through the smelly days.

The daffodils hung their heads, sorry to see him go. Digger sniffed and gave a last little wave of his tail before he disappeared down the drive.

He had not gone far when he heard something behind him. He turned around, to find Myrtle, Dragonfly and Gecko following him. Worm had come along for the ride.

"Digger, Digger! Don't run away," buzzed Dragonfly.

"We would all miss you!" cried Gecko.

"Especially Joyce," said Worm.

"Oh why can't you and Myrtle be mates?" asked Gecko.

"Thanks very much," Digger replied, stiffening his tail, "but there isn't room for both me and that wombat." He crossed the road and kept walking.

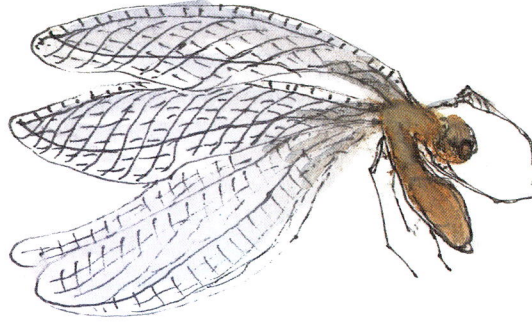

Myrtle waddled along after him, her little legs finding it hard to keep up. She did not see the big truck as it thundered round the corner.

"Look out!" cried Dragonfly. But Myrtle had already disappeared behind the big black tyres.

Everything was quiet. Even the kookaburras were silent. They stared at the little wombat lying still in the road.

"Poor Myrtle," hummed Dragonfly. "It was her idea to bring you home."

"She wanted me home?" Digger's tail drooped. He padded over to where Myrtle lay. He touched her gently with his paw.

Myrtle's eyes opened.

"She's alive!" Digger barked with joy. "The tyres missed her. She was only stunned. Oh Myrtle, I can't tell you how pleased I am that you're not squashed."

Myrtle looked up and gave him a big wombat grin.

"Let's go home," buzzed Dragonfly.

Worm was so excited, he had got himself into
a knot. They waited for him to undo himself.
He wriggled onto Gecko's back and cried
"Giddy up!"

And they all marched home together.

Digger decided it wasn't such a bad thing to have a friend to play with, especially one who was such a good digger. At night they would go out digging together: flower beds, rubbish, floorboards . . . nothing was safe!

One day, when Myrtle got locked in the storeroom, she dug her way out through the mudbrick wall. Digger thought this was particularly clever. Joyce was not so impressed.

Myrtle and Digger became good mates.

Though they were friends, Myrtle would sometimes wander off into the bush on her own. As time passed, she would go more often, especially at night. Sometimes she wouldn't come back for days.

"Why does she stay away from home for so long?" Digger asked Gecko.

"The bush is her real home, Digger. She's nearly two years old now and she would probably like a mate of her own kind, a wombat mate."

The days became weeks and Digger's mate did not return. One day, just before sunset, Digger was walking along the road looking for her.

Dragonfly crashed into the bushes. "Don't worry, Digger. Myrtle's gone back to the bush. It's where she belongs."

Digger nodded sadly. He would miss her.

"She'll be all right," hummed Dragonfly.

Digger watched as a car raced up the road. "I hope so," he said softly.

A gust of wind carried Dragonfly up into the fading sunlight. He vanished into the early evening sky. Digger remembered what the daffodils had said. "Perhaps it's true," he thought, "that no one owns the wild things."

With a little wag of his tail, he trotted home to Joyce.

For Hamish and Nicholas Lunn

Acknowledgements
Thanks to Joyce Wilson, whose kindness to an orphaned
wombat inspired this story, and to Naomi Tippett, whose idea
it was to write it. H.L.

Publishers' notes
*Very sadly for all who were involved in this book, it turned out to be
Clifton Pugh's last work – for art and for conservation. The book
stands as a tribute to his concern that children have access to both art
and ideas about our natural environment, though he was unable to
see the book through to publication.*

*Digger's Mate is based on the true story of an orphaned wombat
being raised in the same household as a dog. Usually dogs are
dangerous to wildlife and should be kept away from baby animals –
but this was an unusual true story.*

National Library of Australia
Cataloguing-in-publication data
  Lunn, Helen, 1963-
  Digger's Mate
  ISBN 0 947214 16 X (hdbk)
  ISBN 0 947214 17 8 (ppbk)
  I. Pugh, Clifton, 1924-1990. II. Title
  A823'.3

AIRD BOOKS PTY LTD
P.O. Box 122
Flemington
Victoria 3031
Australia

First published by Aird Books in 1991
Copyright text © Helen Lunn, 1991
Copyright illustrations © Clifton Pugh, 1991

Consultant publisher: Jackie Yowell
Designer: Paul Barnett

Typeset in Bembo Roman
by CAPS & lowercase
Printed by Allanby Press, Melbourne